3-Minute Stories

Bedtime Tales

publications international, ltd.

CONTENTS

Rip Van Winkle

Adapted by Pegeen Hopkins
Illustrated by John Lund

If the legends of old are true, there is a touch of magic in the Catskill Mountains. Many years ago, a simple, friendly man lived in a town at the base of those mysterious mountains. His name was Rip Van Winkle.

Rip had a wife and several children. He was a kind neighbor, loved by everyone in town. When he walked through the streets, children asked for piggyback rides. Even the neighborhood dogs loved him.

One afternoon, Rip Van Winkle wandered to the top of one of the highest mountains. Suddenly he heard someone call his name. He turned and saw no one.

"Rip Van Winkle," he heard once more. Rip looked around again. This time, his eyes fell on a strange little man climbing toward him.

On his shoulder, the little man carried a huge barrel. "Would you help me with this?" the little man asked.

"Of course," Rip replied. They soon entered a large clearing, where Rip saw a strange group of little men. When Rip and the little man reached the group, one man took the barrel from Rip's hands and poured a dark liquid into a strange cup. The men motioned for Rip to drink it.

Once Rip had finished several cups, he felt tired. His eyes drooped, his vision blurred, and he drifted off into a deep sleep.

When Rip finally opened his eyes, it was morning. Rip was lying right where he had been when he first met the little man.

"Have I been asleep here all night?" Rip exclaimed in a panic. "Mrs. Van Winkle is going to be so angry! What will I tell her?"

Rip started down the mountain feeling a bit confused. As he got to his village, people looked at him with surprise. No one in town looked familiar to Rip. The people did not know Rip, and he did not know them.

Finally, Rip looked down to see what everyone was staring at. A long beard flowed down to his knees!

"Does anybody here know Rip Van Winkle?" Rip asked a group of people.

A tall man asked Rip, "Just exactly who are you?"

"I was myself," Rip said. "I fell asleep on the mountain. Now everything has changed."

Right then a young woman came forward. Rip was sure he had seen her face before, but she had grown up. "What is your father's name?" Rip asked.

"Oh, Rip Van Winkle was his name," said the woman. "It has been twenty years since he took off into the mountains. We have heard nothing about him since."

Rip Van Winkle

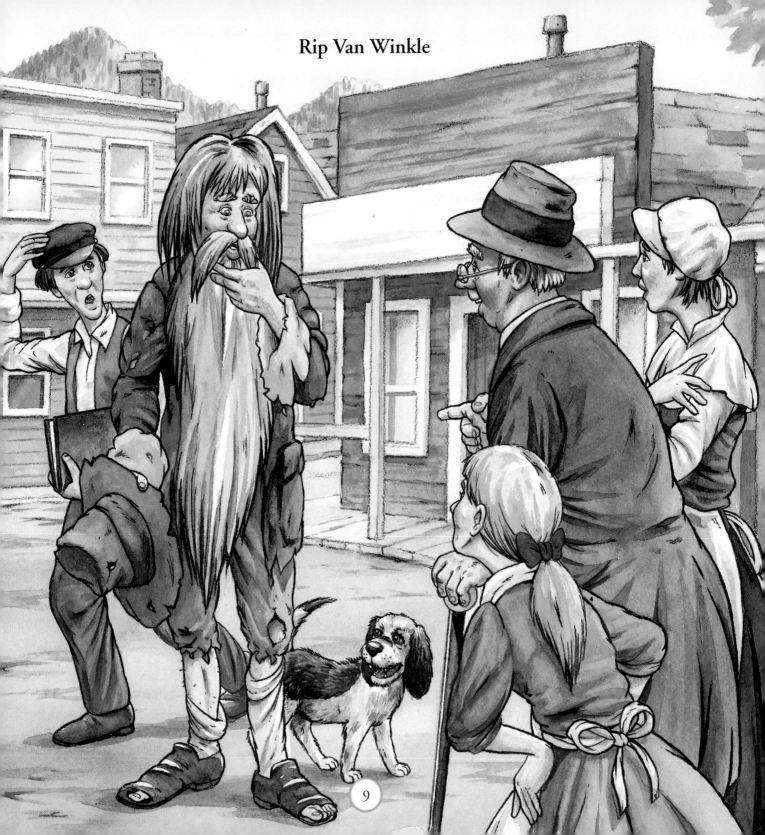

9

"And what about your mother?" Rip asked.

"She just recently passed away," said the woman. Hearing this, Rip could no longer contain himself. "I am your father," he cried as he hugged her. "Once I was young Rip Van Winkle. Now I am old Rip Van Winkle. Doesn't anyone know me?"

An old woman walked right up to Rip and put her face almost against his so she could see clearly. "Sure enough," said the old woman. "Welcome home, Rip Van Winkle. Where have you been all these years?"

It did not take Rip long to tell his story. He could not believe he had missed watching his children grow. His wife was dead now. Much of his life had passed in one night. The townspeople listened, amazed. Some people regarded old Rip Van Winkle as the unluckiest man in town. But other people did not believe that a man could sleep for twenty years. Do you?

Little Red Riding Hood

Adapted by Lisa Harkrader
Illustrated by Wendy Edelson

nce upon a time there was a little rabbit who
always wore a bright red cloak with a hood. Her
as Little Red Riding Hood.

y Little Red Riding Hood and her mother
asket full of good things to eat. They filled
andmother's favorite foods, like carrots,
nge blossom honey, and homemade
ads and tarts.

"Take this basket straight to your grandmother's house," said Little Red Riding Hood's mother.

Then with a kiss on the forehead, her mother sent Little Red Riding Hood off through the woods to Grandmother's house.

Little Red Riding Hood had not gone far when a wolf approached her. "Where are you going?" he asked.

"I'm not supposed to talk to strangers," said Little Red Riding Hood.

The wolf looked at her basket. "A picnic?" he asked.

"It's not a picnic," said Little Red Riding Hood as she held the basket close. "It's a basket for my grandmother."

The wolf sniffed the basket to find out what was inside. "No flowers?" asked the wolf. "I would never visit my grandmother without a big bunch of flowers. Perhaps you should stop and pick some for her."

Little Red Riding Hood thought that was a good idea. She picked buttercups and daisies, while the wolf ran down the path toward Grandmother's house.

Grandmother was rocking in her favorite rocker, mending her favorite apron. She did not hear the door creak open. She paid careful attention to her needlework, so she did not see the big, hairy wolf sneak into her little house.

Little Red Riding Hood

The wolf slipped into a closet and waited until he was sure that Grandmother was alone in the house. "Grrr!" snarled the wolf as he sprang from the closet.

"Oh my!" cried Grandmother as she jumped up from her chair and knocked over the table. Grandmother ran out of that house as fast as she could.

The wolf looked through Grandmother's closet and found her nightcap, gown, and some glasses. He put them on, leaped into bed, and pulled the covers up over his nose. Little Red Riding Hood arrived a few minutes later.

"Grandmother, are you home?" she called from the open door.

"In here, my little dumpling," the wolf said softly.

Little Red Riding Hood hurried inside. "Grandmother, what big ears you have!" she said as the nightcap slipped off the wolf's head.

"All the better to hear you with, my dear," said the sneaky wolf. Then Grandmother's glasses slipped down from the wolf's eyes.

"Grandmother, what big eyes you have!" said Little Red Riding Hood.

"All the better to see you with, my dear," said the wolf as he slowly pulled the covers down from his face.

"Oh Grandmother!" said Little Red Riding Hood. "What big teeth you have!"

"All the better to eat you with, my dear!" growled the wolf as he jumped off the bed.

"You're not my grandmother!" screamed Little Red Riding Hood. "Why, you're the big, bad wolf from the forest! What have you done with my grandmother?"

The wolf chuckled. "You will never find out, my dear," he said.

"That's what you think," said someone behind them. Little Red Riding Hood and the wolf turned around. There was Grandmother standing in the doorway with a big, strong lumberjack.

The wolf chuckled again. "One old lumberjack cannot catch a quick and smart wolf like me."

The wolf leaped toward the bedroom window. But he did not get very far.

Little Red Riding Hood quickly grabbed the wolf's tail, while Grandmother snatched her nightcap and pulled it down over the wolf's eyes.

The lumberjack picked up the wolf and carried him off toward the river. Little Red Riding Hood and her grandmother followed closely behind to see what would happen next.

When the lumberjack finally reached the river, he set the wolf down on a big log and quickly pushed it into the water. The wolf sadly sailed away down the river.

Little Red Riding Hood

"He doesn't look so big out there in the middle of that wide river," said Grandmother.

"He doesn't look so bad and mean when he's so far away from us," said Little Red Riding Hood.

"And he doesn't look like he will be coming back anytime soon," said the lumberjack.

With the wolf safely gone, everyone went back to Grandmother's house and enjoyed the food in the basket. As Grandmother sipped some tea, she smiled at Little Red Riding Hood.

"You are very brave," she said. "And I'm glad I'm your grandmother."

From that day on, Little Red Riding Hood never had to worry about the wolf when she traveled through the woods to Grandmother's house.

The Five Brothers

Adapted by Brian Conway
Illustrated by Leanne Mebust

Once there were five brothers who looked exactly alike. They lived with their mother in a little house beside the sea. Their father had been a sorcerer, and the five brothers came to have very special abilities, too.

The first brother could slurp up the whole sea and hold it in his mouth. His skill was most useful when it came time for fishing.

One morning the king wanted to go swimming. But he quickly discovered the water was missing!

"Who has taken the water away?" the king said to his guards. "Go and find him!"

When the first brother saw the king's guards approaching, he quickly tried to put the water back in its place, while his brothers hurried home with their fish.

"How dare you take all of the sea for yourself!" the king scolded. "You will be punished!"

The king ordered his guards to blindfold the first brother, take him deep into the woods, and leave him there. "Please, Your Highness," said the first brother, "allow me to go and bid my dear mother good-bye."

"It is only fair," the king agreed.

The first brother went home and asked the second brother to go back in his place. The guards covered the second brother's eyes. They led him for many miles through the woods, twisting and turning away from any paths, around tree after tree. Then they left him in the forest by himself.

The second brother, who could see through the back of his head, knew exactly where he was and how to get back. Walking home, though, he ran into the guards again. They quickly grabbed him and took him to the king.

"You are clever," said the king, "but I know what to do with you."

The king ordered the guards to lock the second brother inside a box and carry him by buggy to another kingdom. "Please, Your Highness," the second brother pleaded, "allow me to go and bid my dear mother good-bye."

"It is only fair," said the king.

The second brother went home and asked the third brother to go back in his place. The third brother, who could creep through any crack, was locked in a box that was put onto a buggy. As the buggy drove off, standing right there behind two guards was the third brother!

The guards grabbed him and brought him before their king. "I know what to do with you!" growled the king. He ordered his guards to take the third brother out to sea and drop him in the deepest waters.

"Please, Your Highness," said the third brother, "allow me to go and bid my dear mother good-bye."

"It is only fair," said the king. The third brother went home and asked the fourth brother to go back in his place. The guards took the fourth brother to the deepest waters and dropped him in.

The fourth brother could stretch and stretch his legs.

He did just that until his feet touched the bottom of the sea. The fourth brother did not sink! The guards pulled him out of the water and took him to the king. "Take him to the dungeon!" the king shouted.

"Please, Your Highness," the fourth brother pleaded, "just let me go and bid my dear mother good-bye."

"I suppose it is only fair," said the king.

The fourth brother went home and asked the fifth brother to go back in his place. The guards put the fifth brother into the cold dungeon. The fifth brother could spin faster than a top, and he flew up, up, up through the roof above him.

The king was in his bed when the floor began to rumble. The frightened king gasped as the fifth brother came spinning up through the floor!

"How did you do that?" the startled king asked. "You are more than just clever. You are a wizard!" The king then shouted for his guards.

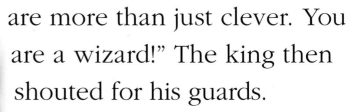

"Please, Your Highness," the fifth brother pleaded. "I am different, it is true. But I have a gift, just like you." The fifth brother pointed at the king's feet.

"What do you mean?" asked the curious king. The king had very large feet, and he was very embarrassed about them.

"Why, your grand feet can be used for a very, very important job in the kingdom, Your Highness," the fifth brother replied. "Making mashed potatoes!"

The king realized that he, too, was able to do something that no one else could do. In minutes, he could make hundreds of pounds of mashed potatoes with his huge feet.

From then on, the king happily showed off his feet each day as he walked barefoot through his kingdom. The five brothers and their mother were happy too. They enjoyed a lifetime supply of mashed potatoes.

The Velveteen Rabbit

Based on the original story by Margery Williams
Adapted by Cynthia Benjamin and Megan Musgrave
Illustrated by Phil Bliss and Jim Bliss

One bright Easter morning, a little boy woke up to find a wonderful basket in his playroom. He was very excited! The basket was full of chocolate eggs and marshmallow treats. But the best present of all was his new velveteen rabbit.

The rabbit's coat was soft, and the insides of its ears were shiny satin. The boy played with his rabbit all day. Soon it was time for dinner, and the boy had to leave his rabbit in the playroom.

Once the boy was gone, the other toys talked to the rabbit.

"I can walk back and forth," said a shiny robot. "Someday I am going to be real. Are you?"

The rabbit turned to Old Horse. He was the oldest and wisest toy in the playroom. "What's real?" asked the rabbit.

"Real is when a child loves you very much for a long, long time," said Old Horse. "It is when he hugs you so much that your shiny coat grows dull and you do not look so new anymore. When you are real you do not care how you look because there is nothing better than being loved."

Soon the boy came back into the playroom.

"Come on, Bunny," said the boy. "It's bedtime." The boy took the rabbit to bed with him and snuggled him close all night. The rabbit felt very warm and cozy.

"This must be what it feels like to be loved," thought the rabbit. "Someday I am going to be real."

One day the boy put the rabbit in his red wagon. "You seem to like that rabbit better than all your other toys," said the boy's mother.

"He's not a toy, he's real," said the boy. The rabbit was so happy to hear this. "The boy really loves me," thought the rabbit. "And now I am real."

The Velveteen Rabbit

The boy soon took the velveteen rabbit on a ride to the woods. When the boy left the rabbit to search for treasures, two furry creatures came out from behind the trees. "What are you?" one of the creatures asked the velveteen rabbit.

"I'm a rabbit, just like you!" said the velveteen rabbit. "Then why can't you move like this?" asked one of the other rabbits as he hopped around. "You're not real."

"Yes I am," said the velveteen rabbit. "The boy told me so." The other rabbits just giggled and hopped away.

As time passed, the velveteen rabbit's fur wore away from being hugged by the boy so much. But the rabbit was happy because he knew the boy loved him.

One day, though, the boy became sick. The doctor told the boy's parents, "You must take your son to the seaside so he can rest and get better."

The boy did not want the velveteen rabbit to get sick, too, so before he went away he left the rabbit under their favorite tree in the woods. "I want you to always remember the wonderful times we had together, Bunny," the boy said sadly.

When the boy went away, the rabbit became very sad, too. He was so sad that he began to cry. A real tear slid down his velveteen cheek.

Suddenly, as the rabbit looked down, a flower grew out of the spot where his tear had fallen.

The blue petals of the flower slowly opened, and out flew a beautiful fairy.

"Do not cry, little rabbit," said the fairy. "I am the fairy of playroom magic. When toys have been loved by a child as much as the boy loved you, I make them real."

"Wasn't I already real?" asked the velveteen rabbit.

"You were real only to the boy because he loved you so much," said the fairy. "Now, because you have been so kind to the boy, and because you truly love him, I will make you real to everyone!"

With that, the fairy gently kissed the velveteen rabbit. "I can move!" cried the rabbit as he started to hop around. "This is so wonderful!"

33

The velveteen rabbit began to leap and jump for joy. "Now I really am real!" he said as he laughed and hopped around some more. Just then, a group of real rabbits gathered around. "Aren't you the same rabbit we saw before?" asked a brown rabbit.

"Yes I am," said the velveteen rabbit. "But now I truly am real! Watch me hop around just like all of you!"

The Velveteen Rabbit

Soon the others asked him to join their group. Away they all ran into the woods, with the velveteen rabbit smiling at his new friends.

Months later, the boy returned to the woods. Suddenly, a rabbit hopped up to him. "You're my velveteen rabbit, aren't you?" asked the boy, as the rabbit winked at him. "I always knew you were real! I will come to visit you as often as I can!"

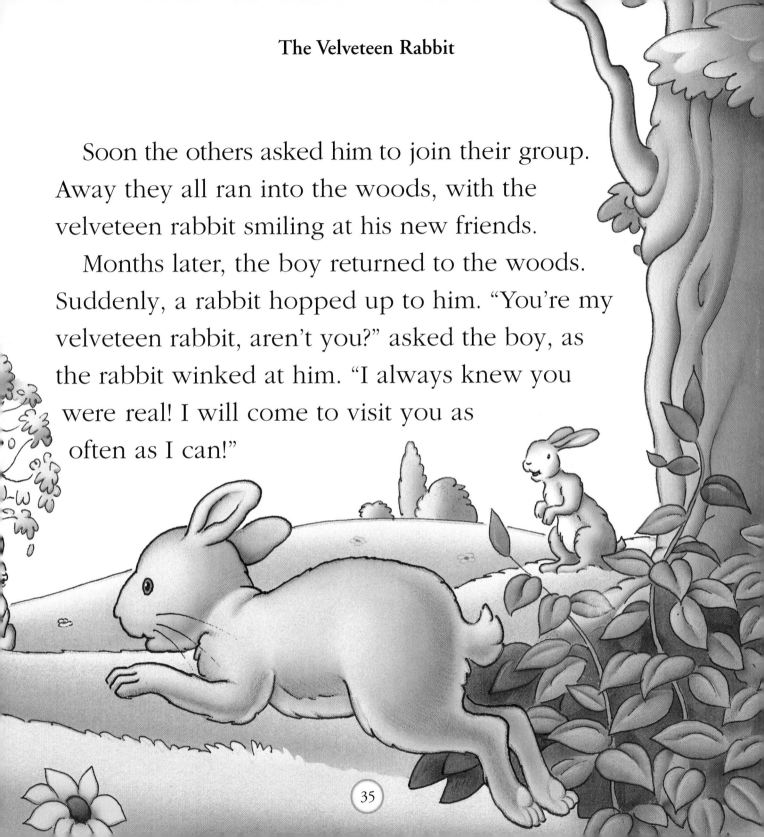

Little Witch

Written by Brian Conway
Illustrated by Leanne Mebust

Little Wanda Witch kept busy studying her big book of magic spells. But she really wanted to play the day away like the other witches did.

Wanda also wanted the other witches to like her. They were older than she was, but they were the only witches to play with. Wanda thought that if she learned all of her witch spells, she could be more like them. Magic spells are never easy, even for a smart little witch like Wanda.

"Abracadabble!" said Wanda. "No, that's not it. Abracabubble! No, that's not right either." Sometimes the spells made Wanda dizzy.

The book was full of tricky tongue-twisting talk. But Wanda was not the kind of witch who gave up easily. Wanda knew she could learn every last trick in that big book of spells.

"Someday," Wanda thought, "I'll be big enough to boil and bubble and all that stuff." And sure enough, Wanda soon was ready for her first witch's trick.

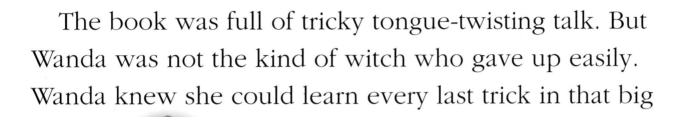

Wanda had practiced the trick over and over again in her mind. Now she would do it for real!

Wanda looked at her book one last time. Then she hopped on one foot and twiddled her fingers, just like her big book of magic spells said. Finally, Wanda began to chant.

"Broom, broom, who needs you? Warty, haggy witches do. You can sweep the floors inside. A tricycle's the thing to ride!"

Wanda felt some magic stirring in the air. She twiddled her fingers again, passing a zap from her hands to the broom.

POOF! It worked! Well, sort of. The broom changed, but not like Wanda wanted it to.

"Oops!" said a disappointed Wanda. "That's not a tricycle. It's an icicle!"

Wanda went back to her book of spells to study some more. "I wonder what went wrong?" said Wanda to her kitten. Wanda looked at her book. "I did everything right. It's the spell that must be wrong."

So Wanda found another spell she could try right away. "I need your help, Kitty," said Wanda. Kitty tried to hide under the table. Kitty liked being a kitty. She did not want to turn into an icicle or a spider.

"Don't worry, Kitty," Wanda assured her. "It's an easy one. Now just stay still."

Just to be safe, Wanda read right from the book this time. In her very best witch's voice, Wanda shrieked, "Abracablue and abracablots! Wouldn't Kitty be pretty with polka-dot spots?"

POOF! This trick worked too, but not like Wanda thought it would. Wanda got lots of spots, it's true, but they were not on her kitten. They were on the polka-dotted puppy dogs all over her bedroom!

Wanda had some troubles, but she would never give up. She shooed the puppies out to some polka-dotted doghouses in the yard, and then she found a toad.

This toad did not have a single wart on his entire body. Wanda felt sorry for the little guy. She knew she had a spell to get his skin as lumpy as it should be.

Wanda clicked her heels, pointed at the toad, and chanted her spell. "Dimples and pimples and bumps of all sorts. A toad's needs are simple — clumps of big warts!"

POOF! Wanda's magic gently zapped the toad. When she saw what had happened, Wanda could not believe her eyes!

Could it be true? Yes! Wanda's spell worked! She hurried out to the cauldron to show the other witches her happy toad.

"I did it! I did it!" Wanda called to the other witches. "It's my first real witch's trick. Look at how lumpy the toad is now."

"Oooh, what marvelous warts," the other witches cooed. "We must have some."

So Wanda tried her wonderful wart trick on the other witches. She knew what had worked the first time, so she did not change a thing this time around.

POOF! The spell worked again! The other witches now had lots and lots of lumpy warts.

But suddenly they were not witches anymore. They had turned into toads! "Uh-oh," Wanda sighed.

Then Kitty brought Wanda her little witch's broom. Wanda finally remembered the first rule of witchery! It was not in any book. Wanda learned it from her mother when she was very small.

"If you find you're in a mess, your little witch's broom's the best. For fixing messes clean and clear, just wave your broom around, my dear!"

Wanda did just that. *POOF*! The warty toads became witches again! And the witches were not mad at Wanda at all. In fact, they thought Wanda was the smartest little witch around.

The Ugly Duckling

Adapted by John O'Grady
Illustrated by Mike Jaroszko

High upon her unhatched egg, the mother duck sat for yet another night. Her duckling was taking its time. The sixth egg was larger than the others. It was a different color, too.

The mother duck spoke to it. "Come now, little one. All of your brothers and sisters are waiting for you!"

With those words, a crack began to grow in the shell of the sixth egg. Then the egg rocked gently.

The mother duck smiled as her last duckling broke through its shell. "Aren't you a large duckling!" she quacked.

"Your neck is so long, and you're not quite as yellow as the others. But I love all six of you the same."

Soon the ducklings waded into the water for their first swim. The large gray duckling was an especially strong swimmer. After days of swimming practice, the mother duck brought her ducklings to meet the other animals. "What have we here?" asked the peacock.

The mother duck said, "This is my youngest."

"He's also the ugliest of your ducklings!" laughed the peacock.

"Yes, my youngest looks a little different," said the mother duck. "But he is my strongest swimmer."

The mother duck gathered her ducklings. "Pay no mind to the peacock," she told them. "Remember, I love all of you the same."

But the ugly duckling felt terrible. That night he decided he must run away and let the rest of his family enjoy the pond without him. When he was sure that everyone was fast asleep, the ugly duckling walked into the night. When the sun rose the next day, the ugly duckling found himself at the edge of a new pond. Geese lived on this pond. "Are you lost, duckling?" one goose asked.

"No, I am not lost," said the ugly duckling. "I have run away from home."

"We were just going to fly away ourselves," said the goose. "You are welcome to fly with us."

The ugly duckling felt very lucky to have met such friends. But just as the ugly duckling started to say he would fly with them, a big, howling dog leaped from the grasses and startled the flock of geese. The geese flew into the air and quickly out of sight.

The ugly duckling hid among the cattails. Afraid to move, he sat there for hours. Day turned into night, and the dog did not return. But neither did the geese.

The geese knew something that the ugly duckling did not. Winter was coming, and they needed to travel to warmer waters. This would be the duckling's first winter.

With winter came wind, ice, and bitter cold. The ugly duckling was also very lonely. More and more, he missed his mother. He also missed his brothers, sisters, and the warm waters of their pond.

One night the ugly duckling had a wonderful dream. A fire warmed his feathers, and walls held off the wind and snow. Not wishing to wake up, the ugly duckling opened just one eye. A cat and a hen were peering at him!

"Where am I?" asked the ugly duckling.

"Our old woman found you," said the cat.

"She brought you home so you could thaw out."

Each day, the ugly duckling sat by the window and watched for signs of spring. Soon he decided it was time to leave. For days the ugly duckling walked and walked, searching for a place where he could rest and stay warm.

Finally he came to a marsh, where he curled up inside a hollow tree. The snow soon melted, the marsh came alive, and birds returned to their nests.

One morning the duckling awoke to find four swans gliding on the water. "Good morning, swans," said the ugly duckling.

"I am sorry to make you look at me," continued the ugly duckling, "but I must swim to find food."

"You are a pleasure to see!" said one of the swans.

"Your feathers are like pure snow, and your neck is so long and graceful," said another swan.

"Please do not mock me," said the ugly duckling.

The largest swan swam to his side. "Open your eyes, friend," said the swan. "We do not mock you."

The ugly duckling glanced at his reflection in the water. It was the most beautiful swan he had ever seen. "That is me?" he asked the large swan.

"Of course that is you," the large swan said gently.

"Where is your family? Why are you alone?"

The beautiful new swan told his tale to the other swans. "And I still miss my mother," he said. "She loved me even when I was an ugly duckling. Now I am afraid I will never see her again."

"We will help you find her," said the large swan.

So the five swans flew off on their search. Soon they reached that special pond where a mother once sat patiently waiting for her eggs to hatch.

"Mother, I'm back home!" said the beautiful swan who was once an ugly duckling. And his mother still loved him just the same, whether he was an ugly duckling or a beautiful swan.

Goldilocks and the Three Bears

Adapted by Jennifer Boudart
Illustrated by David Merrell

There once was a family of three bears. Papa Bear, Mama Bear, and little Baby Bear lived in a cozy cottage right in the heart of the forest.

Each day Mama Bear made three bowls of oatmeal and set them out on the table. While the oatmeal cooled, the Bear family would take a nice walk in the forest. One morning there also was a young girl walking in the forest.

The young girl was named Goldilocks because she had ringlets of golden hair. Goldilocks had wandered into the forest all by herself. She was terribly hungry and tired. Goldilocks walked until she came upon a lovely little house. "Is anyone home?" called Goldilocks. No one answered, so she opened the door and let herself in. Goldilocks saw three bowls of oatmeal on the table. Her stomach began to rumble. "I wish the owners would come home and offer me a bit of oatmeal," Goldilocks thought. She waited a little longer and then reached for a spoon.

Goldilocks dipped the spoon into the largest bowl of oatmeal, which belonged to Papa Bear. "Oh no, this oatmeal is much too hot!" Goldilocks said. She then tried some oatmeal from the middle-size bowl that belonged to Mama Bear. "And this oatmeal is much too cold," she said.

Finally, Goldilocks took a small taste from the little bowl that was set out for Baby Bear. "This is the most perfect oatmeal ever!" she said, and she licked the bowl clean.

Goldilocks felt full after eating the oatmeal. She poked her head into another room of the house and saw three lovely chairs. Goldilocks decided to sit in the big chair that belonged to Papa Bear.

"Oh no, this chair is much too hard!" she said. Then she took a seat in the nice middle-size chair where Mama Bear enjoyed sitting. "This chair is much too soft," Goldilocks said.

Goldilocks moved on to the last chair. It was a tiny rocking chair that Baby Bear loved to rock back and forth in.

"This is the most perfect chair!" said Goldilocks as she laughed with joy.

After a while, Goldilocks tried to squeeze out of the small chair, but she was stuck. She tried to stand up again, but the chair broke into pieces beneath her.

"Oh my!" said Goldilocks. "I have broken the chair. I must wait here for the owners to come home so that I can tell them how sorry I am."

But there was no place left for Goldilocks to sit, so she wandered through the cozy cottage.

Goldilocks came across a lovely room with three beds in a row. She lay on the largest bed, which belonged to Papa Bear.

"Oh no, this bed is much too hard," Goldilocks said. Goldilocks then tried the middle-size bed where Mama Bear liked to rest all winter.

"This bed is too soft!" Goldilocks said. There was only one more bed. Goldilocks lay down in the bed where Baby Bear napped each afternoon.

"What a perfect little bed!" said Goldilocks. Within moments, Goldilocks was sleeping so soundly that she did not hear the Bear family come home.

Papa Bear, Mama Bear, and Baby Bear were ready for breakfast. When they got to the kitchen, they could not believe their eyes!

"Someone has been eating my oatmeal!" said Papa Bear in his loud, rumbly voice.

"Someone has been eating my oatmeal as well," said Mama Bear. "And that someone has left quite a mess!"

Baby Bear went to his bowl of oatmeal. "Someone has eaten *all* of my oatmeal!" cried Baby Bear.

The Bear family walked into their sitting room, and again they were surprised. "Someone has been sitting in my chair, I think!" Papa Bear said in his loud voice.

"Someone has been sitting in my chair as well," said Mama Bear. But when Baby Bear went over to his favorite rocking chair, he found it was broken to pieces.

"Oh my," Baby Bear cried. "Someone has been sitting in my chair, and that someone was very careless."

"Maybe we should check the bedroom," said Mama Bear. The Bear family walked to their bedroom.

"Someone has been sleeping in my bed," said Papa Bear. Mama Bear looked at her middle-size bed. "Someone has been sleeping in my bed too," she said. Baby Bear walked slowly to his small bed and saw what was under the covers. Frightened, he touched Goldilocks gently to see if she was real. He ran to his parents. "Someone has been sleeping in my bed," said Baby Bear. "And that someone is sleeping there still!"

Goldilocks slowly opened her eyes and saw the three bears. Screaming, Goldilocks leaped from the bed.

"Who are you?" asked Papa Bear.

Goldilocks jumped right out the window and ran straight through the forest to her home.

The Bear family would never know who she was or why she had come. Baby Bear sometimes wished she would come back and play, even if that meant sharing his oatmeal.

Puss in Boots

Adapted by Brian Conway
Illustrated by Victoria and Julius Lisi

Puss was a very clever cat. For a long time he belonged to an old farmer. But when the farmer died, Puss could not live on his own. He decided that he would need a new master. Puss went to see the farmer's son.

"I was quite loyal to your father," Puss said, "and he was quite fond of me. If you would be my new master, I promise to serve you just as well."

The farmer's son was very busy with his chores. He did not think he could take care of Puss, too. "If I am going to be your new master, you will have to work for me," said the young man.

"I will work very hard," said Puss. "Just give me a sack and a pair of boots," Puss told the young man, "and you will see how useful I can be."

The farmer's son found a cloth sack and an old pair of boots in the barn. "Let's see what you can do with these," he said.

Puss quickly slid into his new boots. They were sturdy and comfortable. "These will make it easy for me to hunt through the thick brush and mud in the forest," said Puss.

Puss took the empty sack and ran into the woods. "This sack will not be empty for long," Puss called back to his new master. "I will take care of you. You will see."

Before long, Puss had trapped a rabbit inside the sack. Puss carried it to the gates of the palace.

"I would like to see the king," Puss told the palace guard. "Please tell him that I have a gift for him."

Puss was calm and bold in the king's throne room. "Your Royal Highness," he said with a bow, "I offer you a gift from my master."

"What a fine rabbit!" said the king. "I receive many gifts, but this is the finest I have seen in a long time. You are an exceptional cat. Who is your master?"

Puss knew the king would not be impressed with a farmer's son. Puss made up a name, one that sounded very noble.

"My master is the Duke of Carabas," said Puss.

"The Duke of Carabas?" said the king. "I have not heard of him, but please be sure to give him my thanks."

"Indeed, I shall thank him, my king," Puss said as he waved good-bye.

Puss heard about the king's plan to take a carriage ride. The royal carriage would pass by the young man's farm. Puss also learned that the king's daughter, the beautiful princess, would join the king on his ride. Puss rushed home to his master's farm.

The young man was busy with his chores. "Hurry!" said Puss. "Take off your clothes and jump in the river!"

Puss' master was shocked. "Why should I do such a silly thing?" he asked.

"It is for the best," said Puss. "You will see." Puss then gave his master a gentle push into the river just moments before the king's carriage arrived. "Please help!" Puss cried. "The Duke of Carabas is drowning!"

The king remembered the unusual cat. He ordered his guards to stop the carriage.

"My master has been robbed!" Puss told the king. "The thieves took everything and left him to drown!"

The king ordered his guards to pull the young man from the river. Dripping wet and confused, the young man now faced the king.

"At last I meet the great Duke of Carabas," said the king. "Your charming servant has told me so much about you." Puss then bowed politely.

The farmer's son was puzzled. The king ordered one of his guards to return to the palace and bring back a royal suit for the young man. Once the young man changed into the suit, the king said, "Won't you join us on our carriage ride?"

"I would be quite honored," said the young man.

As he climbed into the carriage, the young man saw the beautiful princess. He blushed as he sat beside her.

While the royal carriage rolled along the country road, Puss was still busy with the plans he had for his new master. Puss ran up ahead to a huge castle.

A wicked giant lived in the castle. This giant had magical powers, which he used to scare his neighbors and steal their land.

No one was brave or bold enough to enter the giant's castle. But Puss was not afraid.

Puss walked into the castle and strolled right up to the giant. "What are you doing here?" the giant roared.

"I have heard that you are very powerful," Puss calmly told the giant. "But I do not believe it."

"Huh!" the giant huffed. "I am more powerful than anyone, even the king! I can become a hawk, a wolf, a lion, or a grizzly bear. I can do anything!"

"Only a very powerful giant could change himself into a tiny little mouse," said Puss.

The giant laughed. "That's easy," he said.

The giant shrunk down and became a mouse. Now Puss towered over the giant. Puss pounced on him and popped him into his mouth!

When the royal carriage rode by the castle gates, Puss called out, "Welcome to my master's home!"

"The Duke would be honored if you and your lovely daughter would stay for dinner," Puss told the king.

They all had a wonderful feast, and the princess and the young man got along splendidly at dinner. The princess whispered to her father, "I believe I would like to marry this young man, the Duke of Carabas."

There was a royal wedding the very next day. Puss had taken good care of his new master, so his master took good care of him. Puss had a fine new pair of boots, and he wore them at fancy parties and in royal parades. Exactly where a puss in boots belongs.

Snow White

Adapted by Jane Jerrard
Illustrated by Barbara Lanza

Long ago in a far-off land, a princess was born with skin so pale and lovely that she was called Snow White. As the baby grew into a young girl, she became more and more beautiful each year.

Her stepmother, the queen, was also very beautiful. The queen had a magical mirror, and every day she would look into it and ask, "Mirror, mirror, on the wall, who is the fairest of us all?" The mirror always would answer, "You, my queen, are the fairest in the land." And the queen would be very pleased because she knew that it was true.

But one day, when Snow White had grown to be a young maiden, the queen asked, "Mirror, mirror, on the wall, who is the fairest of us all?" This time the mirror answered, "You, my queen, may lovely be, but Snow White is fairer still than thee."

The queen became very angry because she could not stand to have anyone in the kingdom who was prettier than she. From that day on, the queen hated Snow White.

When the queen could no longer bear to look at the beautiful princess, she called a woodsman and ordered him to take Snow White away from the castle forever. The woodsman took Snow White deep into the dark forest and left her there all alone.

Snow White became very afraid. She heard mysterious noises and saw frightening shadows. Snow White was so scared that she began to run as fast and as far as she could. Finally, she came upon a little cottage.

When no one answered her knocks, Snow White went inside. There she found a little table set with seven plates, and seven little beds were lined up against the wall. The hungry princess nibbled a bit of food from each plate, then she threw herself down on the seventh bed and fell asleep.

Seven dwarfs shared this little cottage. Soon they came back from the gold mine where they worked.

How surprised the dwarfs were to find Snow White sleeping in their home! They let the lovely girl sleep until morning, and then they asked her how she found her way to their cottage deep in the woods. When they heard Snow White's story, they felt sorry for her and asked her to stay.

Snow White took care of the cottage, and the dwarfs gave her food, friendship, and shelter in return. Snow White was happy living with the dwarfs.

But one day back at the castle, the evil queen again asked, "Mirror, mirror, on the wall, who is the fairest of us all?" The mirror replied, "You, my queen, may lovely be, but Snow White is fairer still than thee."

The queen then knew that Snow White was still alive, so she quickly made a plan to get rid of Snow White by herself. The queen soon found out where Snow White was staying, and she went to the dwarfs' cottage disguised as an old woman.

When Snow White saw the old woman at the door, she invited her in. Snow White did not know that the old woman was really the queen. The queen offered Snow White an apple, and when Snow White took a bite, she instantly fell to the floor. The queen had placed poison inside the apple!

With a shriek of laughter, the queen rushed back to the castle. She hurried up the steps and ran to her mirror. Once again the queen asked, "Mirror, mirror, on the wall, who is the fairest of us all?"

This time the mirror replied, "Gone is the beauty of Snow White, and you are the fairest in my sight."

Soon the dwarfs finished their daily work and came back to their cottage. They found Snow White on the floor, but they could not wake her. The dwarfs decided to lay her in a glass case so they could watch over her.

One day a prince came by and saw Snow White lying in the case. She was the most beautiful princess he had ever seen, and he fell in love with her instantly. The prince opened the glass case and lifted Snow White into his arms. As soon as he did this, a piece of the poison apple fell from Snow White's mouth, and she awoke from her deep sleep.

Snow White slowly opened her eyes and looked up at the prince's face. She saw that his eyes were filled with love. At that moment, she too fell in love.

The next day, the queen once again asked her mirror who was the fairest in the land. The mirror answered, "You, my queen, may lovely be, but the bride, Snow White, is fairer still than thee." The queen could only shriek in anger, knowing that she had failed to get rid of Snow White.

That same day the dwarfs danced with joy as Snow White and the prince were married right there in the dwarfs' garden.

The Pied Piper of Hamelin

Adapted by Carolyn Quattrocki
Illustrated by Tim Ellis

Once upon a time, far away and long ago, there was a town called Hamelin. It was a pleasant little town with a river on one side and a high mountain on the other.

One day the people of Hamelin saw that they had a serious problem. Their lovely town was full of rats! Rats were in the trees, the streets, the alleys, the attics, and the cellars. In short, rats were practically everywhere!

Rats went into the kitchens and bothered the cooks. They fought with the dogs and bit the cats. They were so noisy that ladies having their tea together could scarcely hear each other. What on earth were the poor people of Hamelin to do?

The most important man in town was the mayor. He wore a cape made of fine silk and a matching hat. It was his job to see that everything in town ran smoothly.

The mayor had a town council to help him. The mayor and the council met each week at the town hall to talk about all the things that needed to be done. The meetings were festive occasions, and there was always a feast of good food and wine.

One day the townspeople said to themselves, "We have had enough of these rats in our town! The mayor and his council sit and do nothing while the rats are  running around everywhere. Something must be done about this!"

Soon a large group of people gathered in front of the town hall and cried out, "Let us see the mayor!"

In his office the mayor listened to the people's complaints. He knew how awful it was to have rats everywhere in town. But the mayor and his council did not have the slightest idea of how to fix the problem.

Suddenly there was a knock at the mayor's door. The people all turned to see a strange fellow standing there as the door opened. He was wearing a long red cape and a hat with a red feather. He had yellow hair, and a pipe hung from a silk scarf around his neck.

"I am a poor piper," the man said, "but I can rid your town of rats. Would you pay me a hundred pieces of gold to do it?"

"Oh, I would give a thousand pieces of gold to anyone who could rid us of these rats!" exclaimed the mayor. The members of the town council shouted, "Yes, yes! A thousand pieces of gold!"

The pied piper
bowed and then walked
to the town square.

As the pied piper began to
play, everyone was amazed at how beautiful and
sweet the music sounded! Then suddenly, rats came
running toward the pied piper from all directions. Big
rats, small rats, thin rats, fat rats, old rats, and young
rats all came running. Before long, the pied piper had
a whole army of rats marching behind him.

Through the town and to the edge of the river the
rats followed the pied piper. At the river's edge he
paused, but the rats kept going. Without stopping,
every single rat jumped into the river and drowned.

Everyone was astonished. All the rats were gone! The people cheered as the pied piper walked back to the town hall.

"I have come to collect my thousand pieces of gold," the pied piper said to the mayor.

"But sir!" cried the mayor. "That was only a joke! You cannot expect us to pay a thousand pieces of gold for such short work. Here are twenty-five pieces."

"You promised one thousand," said the pied piper.

"All right, here are fifty pieces," said the mayor. "Take them and be gone."

The pied piper became angry. The mayor and the town council had lied to him, and he did not like that at all. The pied piper decided to teach them a lesson. He began to play his pipe again as he walked to the town square.

This time the children of the town heard the music and came running toward the pied piper from all directions. The beautiful music was so sweet to their ears that they could not help themselves.

Little hands clapped to the music. Small feet danced to the merry tune. What a parade they made! A long line of dancing children formed behind the pied piper.

Soon all the children in town were following the pied piper as he led them toward the river. All of the parents suddenly became very afraid.

Would their children jump in the river as the rats had done? Just then, the pied piper made a turn.

Soon the pied piper and the long line of dancing children reached the base of the mountain near the town. The townspeople were amazed as a magic door suddenly opened in the mountainside.

The pied piper led all the children toward the door. The poor people of Hamelin cried as they watched the pied piper lead their children through the magic door, never to be seen again.

The children of Hamelin went to live beyond the mountain in a land that was always filled with happiness and laughter and sunshine. And there definitely were no rats!

The Little Dutch Boy

Adapted by Sarah Toast
Illustrated by Linda Dockey Graves

Long ago there was a boy named Hans who lived with his mother in a pretty town in Holland. The land of Holland is very flat, and much of it is below the level of the sea. The farmers in Holland built big walls called dikes to keep the sea from flooding their land.

One day Hans' mother packed a basket of bread and cheese for Hans to take to their old friend Mr. Van Notten.

After a while, Hare thought "I am so far ahead of Tortoise that I think I'll rest here until he comes along. That will show him how foolish he is to race me!"

Hare stretched out on a very comfortable hammock and enjoyed a few tasty carrots. After he had eaten his fill, he felt sleepy. "Well, I suppose there is no harm in taking a little nap," Hare said to himself, and he soon fell fast asleep.

Meanwhile, Tortoise was happily moving along one step at a time, enjoying the scenery of the race course. After quite some time, he came upon the sleeping Hare. "Hello, friend Owl. Hello, friend Squirrel," Tortoise said quietly, so he would not wake Hare.

Tortoise continued on, enjoying the sun and the warm breeze.

Hours passed as Tortoise crept along, over hills and through the forest. He could see the finish line not far ahead of him, yet Hare still dozed away.

Finally, late in the afternoon, Hare awoke. "Oh my!" said Hare with a start. "How long have I been sleeping? I must get back to the race!"

"You had better hurry if you want to win," hooted the old Owl. "Tortoise passed here hours ago."

Hare was surprised to hear he had been asleep so long. "I'd better get moving!" he said as he darted off in a panic. Hare scampered along, scrambling to make up for the time he had lost because of his nap.

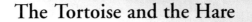

Hare ran and ran. He went as fast as he could, but it was no use. When he ran over the last hill, he could see Tortoise ahead of him, crossing the finish line ever so slowly. "I declare Tortoise has beaten Hare!" shouted Fox.

As the animals cheered for Tortoise, Hare dragged himself to the finish line, out of breath. "How could you have beaten me?" said Hare. "You are so slow and I am so fast!"

"That is right, Mr. Hare," said Tortoise. "I may be slow, but I am steady, and I never stopped going. You see, slow and steady wins the race!"

153

The Three Little Pigs

Adapted by Jennifer Boudart
Illustrated by Judith Mitchell

It was a fine day in the forest. The sun shone brightly through the trees, and its warmth cheered three little pigs who had just left the home they grew up in. The pigs were brothers who hoped to find a new home of their own. A grassy meadow in the middle of the forest seemed to be the perfect spot.

"What a wonderful place to make a new start," said the oldest brother proudly.

"Now that we have found a good spot," said the youngest brother, "let's have lunch." So the little pigs spread out a blanket and ate their lunch while making some plans.

The brothers agreed they should build a house right away. Each brother had a different idea about what kind of house to build. The youngest brother, who was also the laziest, suggested a straw house. The middle brother, who had a bit more sense, thought using wood was a better idea. But the oldest brother made the most sense. "Though it is true, wood is certainly good, bricks are simply the best," he said.

The brothers could not agree. In the end, they decided to build three houses. The youngest brother built his house out of straw, and the middle brother built his out of wood. The oldest brother was the last to finish. While his brothers took naps in the sun, he worked and worked until his brick house was complete, chimney and all.

The brothers had a picnic to celebrate. Proudly, they stood back and admired their three homes.

The three little pigs soon had visitors from all around the forest. One bright morning, the youngest pig heard a knock on his door. Who could it be?

"Let me in," growled a deep voice.

The young pig peeked through a space in the straw wall. A huge, hairy wolf crouched outside his door. He had large teeth, and he looked hungry!

"Not by the hair on my chinny chin chin!" said the young pig.

The wolf snarled. He was very, very hungry.

The Three Little Pigs

"Then I'll huff, and I'll puff, and I'll blow your house down!" roared the wolf.

The wolf let out a blast of air. S-W-O-O-O-S-H! The straw went flying! Then the wolf spotted the little pig pushing himself through the window of the wooden house next door.

The wolf ran to the door of the wooden house. "Let me in!" snapped the angry wolf. Inside the house, the two brothers hugged each other in fear.

"Not by the hair on our chinny chin chins!" they yelled.

"Then I'll huff, and I'll puff, and I'll blow your house down!" roared the big, bad wolf.

Once again, the wolf blew with all of his might. C-R-R-R-A-C-K! All of the boards snapped like twigs.

The little pigs ran to the brick house next door and squeezed down the chimney. The two homeless pigs told their brother about the wolf and their ruined houses. Outside, the wolf licked his lips as he knocked on the door. "Let me in!" he hollered in his meanest, wolfiest voice.

"Not by the hair on our chinny chin chins," said the oldest pig, quietly and calmly.

"Then I'll huff, and I'll puff, and I'll blow your house down!" cried the wolf. He blew his biggest breath yet, but the house was still standing! The wolf blew again. Not a single brick budged!

The pigs heard the wolf jump on the roof. Quickly, the oldest brother lit a fire in the fireplace. Then he sat down to warm his hands.

With a giant crash, the wolf fell down the chimney and landed in the flames. "Let me out!" howled the wolf as he ran in circles. And that's just what the three little pigs did. The wolf ran off and never bothered any of them again.

The three brothers still live in the middle of the forest. They still have picnics and take turns visiting each other's homes. But all of their houses are now made of brick.

The End

Mr. Van Notten lived outside of town, and it was a long way to his house. Mr. Van Notten had only an old dog to keep him company, so he was very happy when Hans came to visit him. To get to Mr. Van Notten's home, Hans just followed the main road out of town. This road ran right alongside a dike.

Hans was very hungry after his long walk, so Mr. Van Notten set out the bread and cheese from the basket and made some cocoa.

After their meal, Hans noticed that the sky had become dark and stormy. He decided that he should leave right away to get home before it started to rain.

Hans walked quickly, but it was not long before cold, stinging raindrops battered him as he struggled against the powerful wind. Hans had no idea he was nearing the town until he saw the dike. It meant he would soon be home.

Hans noticed a small hole in the dike and a trickle of water seeping through the stones. He knew the storm must have whipped up the waves of the sea, and the water had made a crack in the dike.

The Little Dutch Boy

"The dike is breaking!" Hans shouted, but no one heard him. All the windows in the houses had been shuttered because of the storm.

Hans knew that if the hole in the dike got big enough, the sea would surely push its way through and all would be lost. The sea would flood the farms and wash away the little town.

Hans quickly came up with a plan. He balled up his fist and pushed it into the hole. Suddenly, the steady stream of water stopped! Hans was very proud and happy that one small boy could hold back the sea.

Hans was sure his worried mother would soon send people to look for him. But minutes turned into hours.

As darkness fell, Hans became very cold and tired, and his arm began to ache. He had to force himself to keep standing on his tired legs. To keep himself going, Hans thought about how important it was to hold back the water of the sea.

As Hans stood in the cold rain by the dike, he thought about the warmth of the fireplace at home. Then he thought about how good it was going to feel to lie down in his snug bed. These thoughts helped the exhausted boy get through the long, cold night.

When Hans did not come home that evening, his mother began to worry. Even while the rain was falling, she kept looking out the door for Hans to come back. At last she decided that Hans must have waited out the storm at Mr. Van Notten's house. She thought he must have spent the night there because it was too dark to come home after the storm.

After looking out the door one more time, Hans's mother closed up the house and went to bed.

But Hans' mother could not sleep. She was too worried about her son.

Early the next morning, Mr. Van Notten decided to take a walk to Hans' home. He wanted to thank Hans' mother for the tasty food.

Soon Mr. Van Notten came upon Hans. The boy was cold and trembling, and his arm hurt from keeping his fist in the hole in the dike all night.

Mr. Van Notten could not believe his eyes! He told Hans to hold firm for just a little while longer. Then Mr. Van Notten ran toward the town to get help.

Soon Mr. Van Notten returned with someone to take care of Hans and some materials to repair the dike. Hans was wrapped in blankets and carried home. His mother was so happy to see him!

She put Hans in his bed and gave him warm broth to eat, and the town doctor came by to check on him. Hans was all right, but he was so tired that he fell asleep right away and did not wake up until the following day.

Everyone in town came to thank Hans for holding back the mighty sea. The mayor presented Hans with a medal, and all the people cheered! Hans would forever be remembered as a hero.

Patch's Lucky Star

Adapted by Brian Conway
Illustrated by Loretta Lustig

Patch was a pretty little turtle who lived by the pond. She was as quiet and careful as a turtle could be. Most turtles her age romped along the shores of the pond all day, but Patch did not.

Patch looked just like any other young turtle she knew, except for one thing. She had a yellow patch on the outside of her shell. Patch was the only turtle at the pond to have such a shell. "It is such an odd shell for a turtle to have," Patch thought to herself.

"It's not odd," Patch's mother would tell her. "It's just different. It makes you special."

Patch did not want to be special. She just wanted a normal shell so everyone would stop looking at her patch.

Patch would hide away most of the day in the tall grass. She would go to her favorite spots on the pond only when she knew no one was around.

Most days, Patch just tucked herself up inside her shell and stayed there. Patch liked staying inside her shell very much. It was dark and quiet, and Patch could be all alone.

Most of all, though, Patch did not want to have to look at her own shell. She thought the big yellow patch was terrible. In fact, she thought it made her whole shell look terrible. So Patch stayed inside her shell.

One day, Diamond and Snapper walked by Patch's hiding place. They came up and tapped on her shell.

"Patch!" they called. "Come exploring with us." But Patch just stayed very still in her shell. Soon, Diamond and Snapper went away.

Later that day, Patch heard her mother's voice outside her shell. Poking her head out, Patch was surprised to see Diamond and Snapper's mother there, too.

"Have you seen Diamond or Snapper?" Patch's mother asked. "They've been gone for several hours."

"They went exploring," Patch told her mother.

Diamond and Snapper's mother shook her head. "We'll have to go looking for those two," she said. "It is getting dark."

"You stay here, Patch," her mother said. "We do not need another lost turtle."

Patch shivered, glad she had stayed inside her shell. She thought it must be scary to be lost on the pond at night. Then she saw that the stars were starting to glitter in the sky.

"If only my shell could shine as brightly as the stars," she thought aloud. "Then I wouldn't mind my patch so much."

As Patch sighed, she heard Diamond and Snapper calling for their mother. Their mother called back to them. Their voices were coming closer to Patch's place on the shore.

Patch quickly ducked back into her shell. Soon it seemed that all the turtles were just outside, huddled around her.

Everyone was talking all at once. "We kept going in circles," said Snapper.

"Everything looked the same in the dark," said Diamond. "But then we saw Patch's bright yellow patch all the way across the pond."

"We followed Patch's patch all the way back!" said Snapper.

"If you ever get lost again," said Diamond and Snapper's mother, "be sure to follow the bright North Star."

"We don't need the North Star," Diamond and Snapper said. "We've got our own star right here on the shore, and it's the brightest star on the pond, that's for sure!"

"Patch, they're talking about your special shell!" said Patch's mother.

Patch had never been so happy. She popped her head out so she could look back at her patch. In the moonlight, it shined very brightly.

From that day on, Patch loved to look at her shell. She hoped her star would shine all the time. It was a very special patch indeed.

Henny Penny

Adapted by Carolyn Quattrocki
Illustrated by Tim Ellis

One fine day Henny Penny was eating corn, when *boink*! An acorn suddenly fell off a tree and hit Henny Penny right on the top of her head.

"Oh my!" cried Henny Penny. "The sky is falling! I must go and tell the king!"

So Henny Penny tied a nice scarf around her head and set off down the road to tell the king that the sky was falling. On her way she passed the house of Cocky Locky, who was working hard to build a new porch. "Henny Penny, where are you going?" he asked.

"Cocky Locky, the sky is falling, and I am going to tell the king!" said Henny Penny.

"How do you know it is falling?" asked the friendly Cocky Locky.

"I saw it with my own eyes and heard it with my own ears," said Henny Penny. "And a piece of it fell on my head!"

"Then I will go with you to tell the king," said Cocky Locky. Henny Penny and Cocky Locky soon came across Ducky Lucky, who was enjoying a morning swim. "Good morning, Henny Penny and Cocky Locky," said Ducky Lucky. "Where are you going?"

"The sky is falling, and we are going to tell the king," said Cocky Locky.

"How do you know the sky is falling?" asked Ducky Lucky.

"Henny Penny told me," said Cocky Locky.

"I saw it with my own eyes and heard it with my own ears," said Henny Penny. "And a piece of it fell on my head!"

"Then I will go with both of you to tell the king," said Ducky Lucky.

Henny Penny, Cocky Locky, and Ducky Lucky went along until they met Goosey Loosey at the market. "Good morning, Henny Penny, Cocky Locky, and Ducky Lucky," said Goosey Loosey. "Where are you going?"

"The sky is falling, and we are going to tell the king," said Ducky Lucky.

"How do you know the sky is falling?" asked Goosey Loosey.

"Cocky Locky told me," said Ducky Lucky.

"Henny Penny told me," said Cocky Locky.

"I saw it with my own eyes and heard it with my own ears," said Henny Penny. "And a piece of it fell on my head!"

"Then I will go with all of you to tell the king," said Goosey Loosey.

Henny Penny, Cocky Locky, Ducky Lucky, and Goosey Loosey all went along until they met Turkey Lurkey as she was walking through her garden gate.

"Good morning, Henny Penny, Cocky Locky, Ducky Lucky, and Goosey Loosey," said Turkey Lurkey. "Where are you going?"

"The sky is falling, and we are going to tell the king," said Goosey Loosey.

"How do you know the sky is falling?" asked Turkey Lurkey.

"Ducky Lucky told me," said Goosey Loosey.

"Cocky Locky told me," said Ducky Lucky.

"Henny Penny told me," said Cocky Locky.

"I saw it with my own eyes and heard it with my own ears," said Henny Penny. "And a piece of it fell on my head!"

"Then I will go with all of you to tell the king," said Turkey Lurkey.

They all went along until they met Foxy Loxy. "Good morning," said Foxy Loxy. "Where are you going?"

"The sky is falling, and we are going to tell the king," said Turkey Lurkey.

"How do you know the sky is falling?" asked the clever Foxy Loxy.

"Goosey Loosey told me," said Turkey Lurkey.

"Ducky Lucky told me," said Goosey Loosey.

"Cocky Locky told me," said Ducky Lucky.

"Henny Penny told me," said Cocky Locky.

"I saw it with my own eyes and heard it with my own ears," said Henny Penny. "And a piece of it fell on my head!"

"Then come with me," said Foxy Loxy. "I will show you a shorter way to the king's palace."

They all followed Foxy Loxy, and soon they came to the entrance of a dark cave. What they did not know was that this dark cave was really Foxy Loxy's home!

"Just follow me through here," said Foxy Loxy, "and we will soon be at the king's palace."

Henny Penny, Cocky Locky, Ducky Lucky, Goosey Loosey, and Turkey Lurkey all followed Foxy Loxy into the cave. Henny Penny was last in line, and she was frightened. She started to run away.

Henny Penny ran and ran as fast as her legs would carry her. She ran back along the long road. She ran across the narrow bridge. And she ran down the steep hill.

Henny Penny

Henny Penny quickly ran past Turkey Lurkey's garden. She ran past the market where Goosey Loosey had been buying some food. She ran past Ducky Lucky's pond, and she ran past Cocky Locky's house.

Henny Penny ran and ran until, up ahead, she saw her cozy little house with the oak tree beside it. She could even see the corn scattered on the ground underneath the tree.

Henny Penny ran all the way home! She was last seen scratching happily for corn in her little yard.

And the king never did hear from Henny Penny or anyone else that the sky was falling.

The Three Billy Goats Gruff

Adapted by Carolyn Quattrocki
Illustrated by Tim Ellis

Once there were three Billy Goats Gruff. The oldest was Big Billy Goat Gruff, who wore a collar of thick black braid. Middle Billy Goat Gruff had a red collar around his neck, and Little Billy Goat Gruff wore a yellow one.

Big Billy Goat Gruff had a deep billy goat voice. Middle Billy Goat Gruff had a middle-size billy goat voice. And Little Billy Goat Gruff had a very high billy goat voice. All winter long the three of them lived on a rocky hillside.

Every day during the cold winter months the three Billy Goats Gruff played among the rocks. Little Billy Goat Gruff would call out in his little billy goat voice, "Watch this!" as he leaped over little rocks. Middle Billy Goat Gruff would shout, "Watch this!" as he leaped over middle-size rocks. Big Billy Goat Gruff would bellow in his big billy goat voice, "WATCH THIS!" as he leaped over great big rocks.

One night a strong, cold wind was blowing. Big Billy Goat Gruff said, "It is time for us to find a warm place to stay." So the three Billy Goats Gruff found a nice, cozy cave to sleep in. During the cold nights they dreamed of springtime.

When spring finally arrived, the three Billy Goats Gruff looked longingly across the rushing river. "How I would love to go up the mountains on the other side of the river," said Little Billy Goat Gruff.

"The grass is green, and the flowers are pretty. There is plenty to eat on that side."

"To get to the mountains," said Middle Billy Goat Gruff, "we will have to cross the bridge over the river." The three Billy Goats Gruff knew that a mean, ugly troll lived under the bridge. The troll had eyes that were as big as saucers, a head of shaggy hair, and a nose that was as long as a flute.

One day Big Billy Goat Gruff thought of a plan to trick the troll so they could cross the bridge. The next morning the three Billy Goats Gruff went down to the river. Little Billy Goat Gruff started to cross the bridge. *Trip-trap, trip-trap, trip-trap* went Little Billy Goat Gruff's feet on the wooden bridge.

"Who's that *trip-trapping* across my bridge?" roared the troll.

"It is only I, Little Billy Goat Gruff," said the little billy goat.

"I'm coming to eat you up!" hollered the troll.

"Oh no!" cried Little Billy Goat Gruff. "I am only a tiny, little billy goat. Wait for my brother, Middle Billy Goat Gruff. He will make a much bigger dinner for you to eat." So the troll let the little goat go across.

When Middle Billy Goat Gruff started to cross the bridge, the troll hollered, "I'm coming to eat you up!"

"Oh no!" cried Middle Billy Goat Gruff. "I am only a middle-size billy goat. Wait for my brother, Big Billy Goat Gruff. He will make a much bigger dinner for you to eat." So the troll let Middle Billy Goat Gruff cross the bridge to the other side.

Finally, Big Billy Goat Gruff came to the bridge.

TRIP-TRAP, *TRIP-TRAP*, *TRIP-TRAP* went Big Billy Goat Gruff's feet as he walked across the bridge.

"Who's that *TRIP-TRAPPING* across my bridge?" roared the troll.

"It is I, Big Billy Goat Gruff," said the billy goat.

"I'm coming to eat you up!" hollered the troll.

"Come ahead!" said Big Billy Goat Gruff. So the troll climbed up onto the bridge and came toward Big Billy Goat Gruff.

Suddenly, Little Billy Goat Gruff and Middle Billy Goat Gruff called out from the other side of the bridge. "Look out, troll!" they hollered.

The troll quickly turned toward the smaller billy goats. Suddenly, Big Billy Goat Gruff, with his two big horns, tossed the troll high into the air!

The troll fell swiftly down into the river below with a huge splash.

Big Billy Goat Gruff happily joined Little Billy Goat Gruff and Middle Billy Goat Gruff on the other side of the bridge. There they feasted on the green grass and the wildflowers. From then on, they could cross the wooden bridge whenever they pleased.

Little Ant Goes to School

Adapted by Brian Conway
Illustrated by Richard Bernal

Little Andy Ant used to spend each day with his pull toy, happily playing outside in the warm summer sun. Then, as the summer days got shorter, the sun did not feel so warm anymore.

"Summer is over," Andy's mother told him. "That means today is your first day of school!"

Andy had heard about school. He did not want to be cooped up inside all day long.

School was a strange new place. Little Andy Ant was not ready to go. He was scared and a little sad. Then he thought of an idea.

"Can I take my toy along with me?" asked Andy.

116

"School is for children," his mother answered, "not for toys."

Little Andy Ant tried to be brave. His mother walked him to school that day. "Maybe school won't be so bad once you give it a try," she said. So Andy agreed to try school for just one day.

At school Andy had his very own desk. Teacher gave the children lots of things to do.

Everybody got their own paper and pens. Then they learned all about reading and writing.

Soon Andy started to think about all sorts of new and exciting things.

"Ants work together to make anthills," Andy said to Teacher. "And I think letters work together the same way to make words."

Teacher said Andy was right! He was pretty good at drawing and painting and numbers, too.

Little Andy Ant strolled home from school after a long day. Learning new things was fun!

"Maybe you were right," little Andy Ant told his mother. "Maybe school is not so bad after all."

Andy decided to try school for one more day.

The morning passed by quickly for Andy. Before he knew it, it was already lunchtime. The lunch lady called out, "Cookies and milk!"

What a commotion that caused! Little Andy Ant squeezed his way through and got one tiny chunk of a cookie. Then Andy knew what all the fuss was about. The lunch lady made the best cookies he had ever tasted!

At the end of the day, Andy walked home from school. "Maybe you were right, Mom," said Andy. "Maybe school is not so bad after all."

Andy thought he would try school for another day.
As soon as he arrived at school, Teacher told everyone
that they were going to the woods on a field trip.

Andy learned about new plants and berries at every
turn. Some older children wanted to make a campfire
with their teacher, but they needed Andy's help.

"I know how to get the best twigs," Andy said. He
whistled for his friend Tweeter Bird.

Tweeter Bird brought back the
finest twigs in the woods. There
were enough twigs to build a
campfire and for each little
ant to roast a marshmallow.

Everyone liked Andy and
his friend Tweeter very much.
Andy had a big smile on his
face when he walked home.

Andy not only had his own desk at school, but there were things like field trips and recess, too!

"Maybe you were right, Mom," said little Andy Ant. "Maybe school is not so bad after all."

The next day, Andy wanted to try school again. He did not know what to expect in school that day, but he had an idea it might be fun.

Little Andy Ant walked to school and sat down at his desk. One of the children in his class turned to Andy and said, "I would like you to come to my birthday party today."

After school, Andy raced home. Up until then, he thought birthdays only happened once a year, when he celebrated his own birthday.

Now Andy learned he could celebrate his birthday *and* his friends' birthdays, too!

"I think you were right, Mom," said little Andy Ant. "Maybe school is not so bad after all."

Andy had fun at his school friend's party. He ate some delicious birthday cake and even got seconds!

Little Andy Ant could not wait to get to school the next day! He wanted to learn how to count up to really big numbers, like how many birthdays his class would have.

One day Andy made up a new game for his friends during recess. They all got to swing on the vines!

Everyone looked up to Andy as the most fun ant in their class. "You're the best, Andy!" the children shouted.

Little Andy Ant rushed home after another fun day and told his mother, "School is the best!"

Birthday Cake Mix-Up

Written by Lisa Harkrader
Illustrated by Sherry Neidigh

Barry Bumblebee sat straight up in bed. He rubbed his eyes and looked out the window.

Oh no!" cried Barry. "The sun is up! I'm going to be late for work!"

Barry was the owner of the Busy Bee Bakery. Barry had to go to work before most bugs in town were even awake. The bakery made the most delicious baked goods in town.

Barry pulled on his white apron and baker's hat. Then he rushed out the door of his house.

When Barry arrived at the bakery, his helpers were already busy. Two bees sifted flour while another bee measured cinnamon for a batch of sticky buns. Three other bees mixed batter for the blueberry muffins. "I see we have cherry popovers in the oven," Barry said to his helpers.

Barry continued, "The only things left to make are raisin bread and chocolate chip cookies. I will make those myself."

Barry reached in his pocket for his glasses, but they were not there. "Oh no!" cried Barry. "Now where did I leave my glasses?"

The bakery would be opening soon. There was no time for Barry to look for his glasses!

126

"I bake things every day," said Barry. "Maybe I don't need my glasses."

Barry set out two mixing bowls. He measured the ingredients for cookies with one hand and mixed bread batter with another. Then he poured some raisins into the bread batter and some chocolate chips into the cookie dough. Now it all was ready for the oven.

127

Soon the oven timer dinged, and Barry squinted at the clock. "Time to take my goodies out of the oven and open the Busy Bee Bakery," said Barry.

Carla and Casey Cricket were the first to arrive at the bakery. "You are just in time to taste some freshly baked treats," said Barry as he gave Carla a slice of bread and handed Casey a cookie.

"Yum," said Carla Cricket. "I've never had chocolate chip bread before."

"I love raisin cookies," said Casey Cricket.

Birthday Cake Mix-Up

"Oh no! I mixed up the ingredients!" cried Barry.

"Don't worry, Barry," said Carla. "These are very delicious treats!"

"Thank you," said Barry. "That makes me feel much better. Now I need to bake a birthday cake for my niece Bibi."

Barry pulled out his cookbook. He squinted at Bibi's favorite cake recipe. "A crate of flour," he read from the recipe.

So Barry dumped a crate of flour into his biggest mixing bowl. "Two dozen eggs," Barry read, and he cracked two dozen eggs and mixed them into the flour. He added the rest of the ingredients, poured the batter into his biggest pan, and set it in the oven.

When the timer dinged, Barry peeked into the oven. "Oh no!" he cried. "This cake is huge! I should have used two eggs, not two dozen, and a cup of flour, not a crate!"

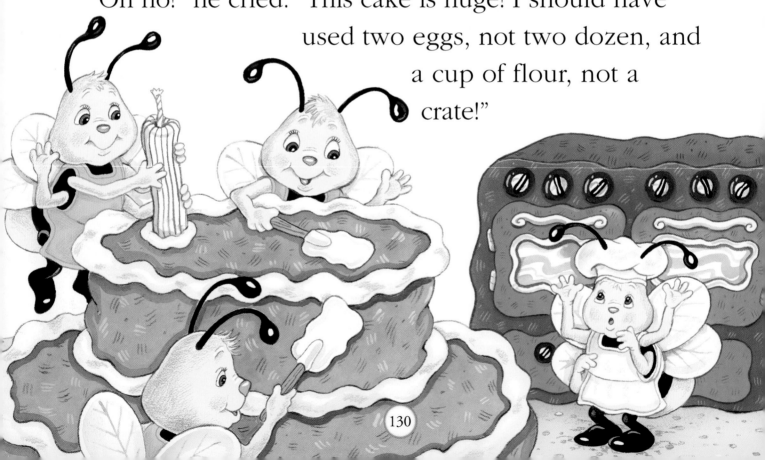

The bees frosted the cake and set it on a cart. Barry rolled the giant cake to Bibi's house. When he arrived, Barry said, "Bibi, I'm sorry."

"For what?" said Bibi as she gave her uncle a big hug. "This is the most wonderful birthday cake I've ever seen!" Bibi's guests began to clap, and Barry sighed with relief. Then Bibi gave her uncle a surprise. "I found your glasses," she said. "I hope you didn't need them at work today!"

Little Red Hen

Adapted by Jennifer Boudart
Illustrated by Linda Dockey Graves

The little red hen lived next to the road by the farmer's house. She shared her home with her five baby chicks and her friends, the dog, the cat, and the duck. The little red hen worked very hard. She kept the house and the yard neat and clean. Everyone liked having a clean house and good food on the table.

When it came time to do the chores, though, the other animals always seemed to disappear. The little red hen did all the work herself.

One day, the little red hen found some kernels of wheat. She showed them to the dog, the cat, and the duck and asked, "Who will help me plant these?" Her three friends looked at the little red hen.

"Not I," said the dog.

"Not I," said the cat.

"Not I," said the duck.

"Then I'll plant them myself," the little red hen told them. Soon her baby chicks came by and told her they wanted to help. The little chicks had lots of fun digging in the dirt.

After a short time they had planted all the kernels. The little red hen visited the garden every day to watch the wheat grow.

One day, she saw many weeds growing in the garden. She found her three friends leaning against the farmer's barn. The little red hen said, "Will you help me pull the weeds?"

"I can't," said the cat. "They're all dirty."

The dog said, "I need to take a nap."

The duck just quacked and waddled off to the pond.

"I'll just do it myself," said the little red hen. Then she walked back to the garden. Once again, her chicks joined her and helped her pull the weeds.

Little Red Hen

A few days later the little red hen worried that the wheat needed more water. She looked for her friends and found them on a pile of hay. The hen said, "Who will help me water the garden?"

The dog, the cat, and the duck looked down at her. "We're busy writing a song and can't be bothered now," said the dog.

"I'll just water it myself," said the little red hen. She took her watering pail to the garden, and her five chicks came to keep her company. For fun, the little red hen sprinkled the chicks with water. Before long, the whole garden had been watered while everyone played.

The summer sun shined almost every day, and the wheat grew fast. Soon it was fall, and the wheat turned golden brown. The little red hen knew what that meant. She found her friends playing cards. The hen asked, "Who will help me harvest the wheat?"

"Not I!" said the dog. "I have good cards."

"Not I!" said the cat. "I'm the dealer."

"Not I!" said the duck. "Wheat makes me sneeze."

"Then I'll harvest it and take it to the mill myself," said the little red hen. She went to the garden, and this time the five chicks were waiting for her. They all cut the wheat together.

Then they took the wheat to the mill. There the friendly miller ground the wheat into flour.

Even though she had already spent a great deal of time and energy on the garden, the little red hen knew there was still a lot more work to be done. She often told her young chicks that if a job was worth doing, it was worth doing well.

The next morning, the little red hen went outside. Her friends were sunbathing on the roof. She called to them, "Who will help me bake bread with my flour?"

The dog, the cat, and the duck did not even bother to look down at the little red hen.

"Not I!" said the dog. "It's a beautiful day. Who wants to be indoors baking bread?"

"Not I!" said the cat. "I have sunbathing to do."

"Not I!" said the duck. "All that flour will get my nice feathers dusty, and I just went swimming!"

The little red hen shook her head. She told the three, "I'll bake it myself," and then she went inside. Her chicks helped her shape the dough into a big loaf.

Soon the smell of baking bread floated in the air. The dog, the cat, and the duck came and looked into the kitchen. The chicks danced around the little red hen. "Who will help me eat this tasty, fresh bread?" asked the little red hen.

"I will!" said the dog, whose tongue was hanging out.
"I will!" said the cat, who licked her whiskers.
"I will!" said the duck, who just stared at the bread.

"Well," said the little red hen, "anyone who helped make this bread can have some. So, if you helped plant the wheat, weed it, water it, harvest it, or bake the bread, raise your hand!"

All five chicks raised their little wings. That night, six tummies got their fill of bread as a reward for work well done. But the dog, the cat, and the duck were left in the yard, where they could feast only on the wonderful smells.

The Lion and the Mouse

Adapted by Sarah Toast
Illustrated by Krista Brauckmann-Towns

One day a lion was taking a nice nap in the warm sun. Nearby, a busy little mouse scurried along looking for berries. But all the berries were too high for her to reach.

Then the mouse spotted a lovely bunch of berries that she could reach by climbing on the rock below them. When she did, the mouse discovered that she had not climbed a rock at all. She had climbed right on top of the lion's head!

The lion did not like to be bothered while he was sleeping. He awoke with a loud grumble.

"Who dares to tickle my head while I'm taking a nap?" roared the lion. The mouse quickly jumped off the lion's head and started to run away.

141

The lion grabbed for the little mouse as quickly as he could, but she was too fast, and he just missed her. The quick little mouse hurried to get away from the lion. She zigged and zagged through the grass, but the lion was always just one step behind. At last the lion chased the mouse right back to where they had started. The poor little mouse was too tired to run anymore.

The Lion and the Mouse

The lion scooped her up in his huge paw.

"Little mouse," roared the lion. "Don't you know that I am the king of the forest? Why did you wake me up from my pleasant nap by tickling my head?"

"Oh please, lion," said the mouse. "I was only trying to get some lovely berries."

"Just see how much you like it when I tickle your head with my big claws," said the lion.

"Please, lion," pleaded the mouse. "If you spare me, I am sure I will be able to help you someday."

The lion stopped suddenly and looked at the mouse. The lion began to smile, and then he began to laugh. "How could you, a tiny mouse, help the most powerful animal around?" he chuckled loudly. "That's so funny. I'll let you go — this time."

Then the lion laughed some more. He rolled over on his back, kicking and roaring with laughter.

The mouse had to leap out of the lion's way to avoid being crushed. Off she ran.

Still chuckling, the lion got up and realized he was hungry. He set out to find some lunch, and it was not long before he smelled food. Walking toward the good smell, the lion got caught in a trap set by hunters.

The lion was stuck in the strong ropes, and the more he wriggled and struggled, the tighter the ropes held him. Fearing the hunters would soon return, the terrified lion roared for help.

The mouse heard the lion's roars from far away. At first she was a little afraid to go back, thinking the lion might hurt her.

But the lion's cries for help made the mouse sad, and she remembered the promise she made to help him. The mouse hurried to where the lion was tangled in the trap.

"Oh lion," said the mouse. "I know what it feels like to be caught. But you do not need to worry. I will try to help you."

"I don't think there is anything you can do," said the lion. "These ropes are very strong. I have pushed and pulled with all my might, but I cannot get free."

"I have an idea!" said the mouse. "Just hold still, and I will get to work." She quickly began chewing through the thick ropes with her small, sharp teeth.

The mouse worked and worked, and before long she had chewed through enough rope for the lion to get out of the trap!

Soon the lion wriggled free. He was very grateful to the mouse. "Mouse," he said, "I thank you for saving me, and I am sorry that I laughed at you before."

"I told you that I would help you someday when you agreed to spare me," said the mouse. "I always keep my word."

Then the lion scooped up the mouse and placed her on his head. He carried her back to the berry bush and lay down under it. "Mouse," he said, "I want you to reach up and pick one of those berries that you wanted earlier today."

The mouse plucked the biggest berry she could find. The lion took the mouse off of his head and held her in his paw.

The Lion and the Mouse

"Let's stick together," he said. "I can help you reach the berries, and you can get me out of a tight spot now and then."

"Okay!" said the mouse. "I will pick you some berries to eat, and we can have a picnic together."

"I don't know if I would like to eat berries, but just having your company would be fine with me," said the lion.

So if you are ever walking along and see a lion laughing and carrying a little mouse, you will know that these two have become great friends because they showed a great deal of kindness to one another.

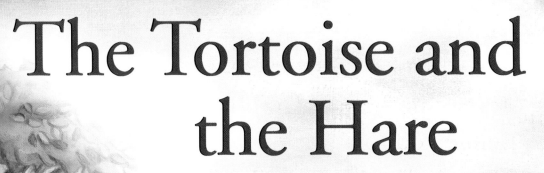

The Tortoise and the Hare

Adapted by David Presser
Illustrated by Viviana Diaz

In the woods there lived a very slow tortoise and a very swift hare. One bright morning, Tortoise was plodding along at his usual pace. Suddenly, Hare came bounding up to him.

"Good morning, Mr. Hare," said the friendly Tortoise. "My goodness, you are moving very quickly today."

"That I am, Tortoise!" said Hare. "But I cannot say the same for you."

"I am a very slow creature," Tortoise said, "but all the same, I would like to challenge you to a race."

"Oh Tortoise!" said Hare. "I could have run a race in the time it took you to make that challenge!"

Then Hare started to laugh so hard that he fell over. Other animals heard the noise. "What's the commotion?" they asked.

"This silly Tortoise has challenged me to a race!" said the Hare. "He is so slow that I won't even have to try hard to win."

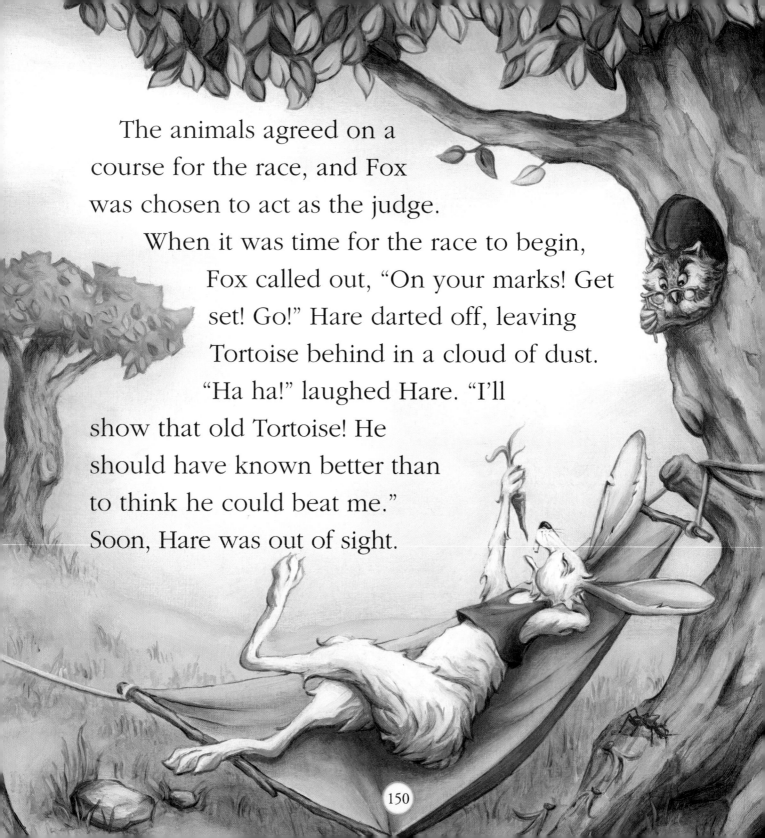

The animals agreed on a
course for the race, and Fox
was chosen to act as the judge.
When it was time for the race to begin,
Fox called out, "On your marks! Get
set! Go!" Hare darted off, leaving
Tortoise behind in a cloud of dust.
"Ha ha!" laughed Hare. "I'll
show that old Tortoise! He
should have known better than
to think he could beat me."
Soon, Hare was out of sight.